PUFFIN BOOKS

Philibert the First and other Stories

Dick King-Smith served in the Grenadier Guards during the Second World War, and afterwards spent twenty years as a farmer in Gloucestershire, the county of his birth. Many of his stories are inspired by his farming experiences. Later, he taught at a village primary school. His first book, *The Fox Busters*, was published in 1978. Since then he has written a great number of children's books, including *The Sheep-Pig,* (winner of the *Guardian* Award and filmed as Babe), *Harry's Mad, Noah's Brother, The Hodgeheg, Martin's Mice, Ace, The Cuckoo Child* and *Harriet's Hare* (winner of the Children's Book Award in 1995). At the British Book Awards in 1992 he was voted Children's Author of the Year. He is married, with three children and ten grandchildren, and lives in a 17th Century cottage a short crow's-flight from the house where he was born.

Other books by Dick King-Smith

BLESSU and DUMPLING
CLEVER DUCK
GEORGE SPEAKS
THE GHOST AT CODLIN CASTLE AND
OTHER STORIES
THE HODGEHEG
A HODGEHEG STORY: KING MAX
THE LAST
THE INVISIBLE DOG
MR POTTER'S PET
A NARROW SQUEAK AND OTHER
ANIMAL STORIES
PHILIBERT THE FIRST AND
OTHER STORIES
SMASHER
THE SWOOSE

Dick King-Smith

Philibert the First
and other Stories

Illustrated by Amanda Harvey

PUFFIN BOOKS

PUFFIN BOOKS

Published by the Penguin Group
Penguin Books Ltd, 27 Wrights Lane, London W8 5TZ, England
Penguin Books USA Inc., 375 Hudson Street, New York, New York 10014, USA
Penguin Books Australia Ltd, Ringwood, Victoria, Australia
Penguin Books Canada Ltd, 10 Alcorn Avenue, Toronto, Ontario, Canada M4V 3B2
Penguin Books (NZ) Ltd, 182–190 Wairau Road, Auckland 10, New Zealand

Penguin Books Ltd, Registered Offices: Harmondsworth, Middlesex, England

First published by Viking 1994
Published in Puffin Books 1996
3 5 7 9 10 8 6 4

Text copyright © Fox Busters Ltd, 1994
Illustrations copyright © Amanda Harvey, 1994
All rights reserved

The moral right of the author has been asserted

Made and printed in Great Britain by Clays Ltd, St Ives plc

Contents

Philibert the First

Felicia was a wonderful country.

Every Monday was a Bank Holiday and no one worked on a day with an S in it (which just left Friday).

It never rained in the daytime but only at night.

There were no traffic problems because everyone rode about (very slowly) on donkeys.

And there were no schools. If you wanted to know something, you asked your mum or dad, and if they didn't know how many beans make five, then neither would you.

Finally, even if they didn't always actually love their neighbours, Felicians were always nice to one another, so that everyone was happy. Except the King.

King Philibert the First of Felicia had everything anyone could want. He had his health and strength, he had a beautiful wife and three handsome sons and three pretty daughters, and a magnificent palace and loads of servants and pots of money and a pet walrus called Norman. What more could any man desire?

Yet King Philibert had become unhappy and not a single Felician knew the reason why, not even the Queen.

'Philibert,' she would say each day. 'Why are you unhappy?' And each day the King would reply, 'I'm sorry, my dear, but I do not know.'

"You do still love me, don't you?" the Queen would say, and the King would answer "Yes, my dear, I do," but oh, how sadly he said it.

It was the same with the little princes and princesses. On Fridays those that could read studied the *Encyclopaedia Felicianica* and those that could only weed worked in the Palace gardens. But on every other day they too asked their father, 'Why are you unhappy, Papa?' and the King would reply, 'I'm sorry, my children, I wish I knew why.'

Everyone else wished so too,

because all of them, right down to the poorest beggar in the streets of the capital, FeliCity, were as happy as larks, while their King was as miserable as sin, with a face as long as a boot.

Only one living creature in Felicia looked as sad as King Philibert, and that was his pet walrus, Norman.

Norman was twelve feet long and so fat that he weighed a ton and a half. Some Felicians on an expedition to Greenland had brought him back as a fiftieth birthday present for the King.

Norman's favourite food was oysters, and every morning King Philibert would feed him dozens of them (except when there was an R in the month, and then Norman had to make do with mussels).

And every morning the King
would pat the walrus on top of his
huge round bald head, and say sadly,
'There, was that nice?' and in reply
Norman would give a deep gurgly
moan that sounded like 'Gloom!'
Then the King and his pet walrus
would stare sorrowfully at one
another, the very picture of unhappiness.

'I never can decide,' said the Queen to the little princes and princesses, 'which looks the more miserable.'

She had of course often consulted the Royal Doctor about the King's condition, but though he had suggested dieting, and exercise, and hot and cold baths, and even taking the day off on Fridays, nothing had worked. Even the Court Jester's funniest jokes could raise no smile on the face of King Philibert the First of Felicia.

One morning as the King finished feeding his walrus with oysters, he said with a sigh, 'Very soon, Norman, I shall be fifty-one, and then it will be a whole year since first you arrived and since last I smiled.'

'Gloom!' answered Norman.

And gloom there was, a day or so later, for the walrus was suddenly taken ill with the stomach-ache. To the one usual word he spoke was added another.

'Doom!' moaned Norman. 'Doom!'

Feeling sadder than ever, the King sent for the Royal Vet.

Now it so happened that the Royal Vet was newly appointed and had never before set eyes on King Philibert, let alone on Norman.

'What seems to be the trouble, Your Majesty?' he asked politely.

'It's Norman,' said the King sadly. 'He has the tummy-ache, poor fellow. This morning he actually refused his food.'

'What food, Sire?' asked the Royal Vet.

'Oysters, of course.'

'In the second week of May?' said the Royal Vet.

'Oh help!' said King Philibert. 'I was thinking it was still April. There's no R in this month.'

'Exactly,' said the Royal Vet. 'No wonder he has the tummy-ache.'

'Doom!' groaned Norman.

'We'll soon put him right,' said the Royal Vet. 'Starve him for a couple of days and then switch to mussels and

he'll be as right as rain.'

The King sighed.

The Royal Vet looked carefully at his royal master.

'Forgive me, Sire,' he said, 'if I say that you do not look as happy as the average Felician. In fact you do not look at all happy. In fact you look downright wretched.'

'I am,' said King Philibert. 'Soon it will be a year since last I smiled.'

The Royal Vet looked extremely thoughtful.

'How long, may I ask,' he said, 'has Your Majesty kept this walrus as a pet?'

'Almost a year,' said the King. 'He was a fiftieth birthday present and soon I shall be fifty-one.'

'That's it!' cried the Royal Vet.

'That's what?' cried the King.

'Gloom!' moaned the walrus.

'Norman,' said the Royal Vet, 'is the cause of Your Majesty's unhappiness. Looking at Norman's gloomy face has made you gloomy too.'

'Must I get rid of him then?' said the King. 'Must Norman go?'

'No, no, Sire,' said the Royal Vet. 'What we must do is to turn Norman into a happy walrus, and I think I know how to do this.'

'How?' asked the King.

'Leave it to me, Your Majesty,' said the Royal Vet.

So King Philibert left it to him.

Thus it was that, some months later, another expedition arrived back from Greenland with another present for the King.

It was another walrus, much like Norman to look at, but smaller. When he saw it, King Philibert looked even sadder than usual.

'If one walrus makes me miserable,' he said, 'what will two do?'

But Norman didn't look sadder than usual. Norman didn't look as sad as usual. Norman didn't look sad at all.

His dull fishy eyes suddenly lit up at the sight of the new walrus, his moustache bristled, his mournful expression turned into a kind of a grin. Then he opened his mouth and out of it came, not the usual 'Gloom!' or 'Doom!' but a happy excited roaring noise that sounded like 'Vroom! Vroom!' as he lumbered forward to touch noses with the newcomer.

'He likes him,' said King Philibert.

'He likes her, you mean,' said the Royal Vet.

'Oh,' said the King. 'I see. You mean . . .?'

'I mean, Your Majesty,' said the Royal Vet, 'that from now on Norman will be a different animal. Just look at him!'

And King Philibert looked at his happy walrus, and a great smile spread over his face. Then he began to chuckle, and then he began to laugh, so loudly that the Queen and the three little princes and the three little princesses and all the members of the

18

Royal Household came running to see what on earth had happened.

Oh, what joy there was throughout the land of Felicia as the glad news of the King's recovery became known!

Happy as the people had thought themselves before, now they were even happier, especially when they learned that in celebration a Royal Decree had been issued, forbidding anyone to work on Fridays.

'Oh, Philibert!' said the Queen when at last they were alone together. 'You do still love me, don't you?'

'Yes, my dear,' said King Philibert the First of Felicia. 'I am very, very glad to say I do. Without the shadow of a doubt we shall live happily ever after.'

And they did.

George Starts School

One morning, not long after George's fourth birthday, his mother was watching him as he sat at the breakfast table, reading the *Financial Times*. His father had just left for work, taking George's eleven-year-old sister Laura with him, to school.

'Just think, George,' said his mother. 'Only two more terms and

20

then you'll be going to school too. You'll be a Rising-Five.'

'I am aware of my age, Mother,' said George, turning a page (with difficulty, for the newspaper was large), 'and sometimes I feel it.'

'You'll like school, won't you, George?' said his mother. George put down the *Financial Times* with a sigh.

'The answer to that question,' he said, 'can only be hypothetical. Whether I shall "like" school, as you put it, has yet to be proven. Judging by what I read of the new curriculum, I shall not.'

'Why, is it too difficult?'

'Too easy,' said George, and he picked up the newspaper once more.

It was his mother's turn to sigh, a sigh partly of resignation to the fact

that George always had the last word,
and partly of pride at her most unusual
son. She sat drinking her coffee and
remembering how fantastically early
George had learned to speak, how
fluent he was in the English language
when less than six months old.
Neither she nor her husband had ever
known (because Laura had never

revealed it) that in fact George was holding long conversations with his sister a mere four weeks after his birth, when he knew a great deal more than she did, including his multiplication tables.

'It's a pity,' she said reflectively, 'that there's a seven-year gap between you and Laura. When you go to primary school, she'll have left.'

'Just as well,' said George.

'What do you mean? Don't you like your sister?'

'Mother,' said George patiently, 'I am in point of fact extremely fond of Laura, but I am perfectly accustomed to doing without her during the day. Things will be no different.'

'Yes, but when Laura's at school, I'm always with you, George. I shan't be then. You'll be all alone.'

'According to Laura,' said George, 'there are a hundred and fifty children at the school which I am to attend, not to mention all the teachers, the secretary, the dinner ladies, the caretaker and the odd-job man. I shall not be alone.'

His mother remembered these last words on the day, eight months later, when she walked, holding George by the hand, through the playground full of hordes of rushing yelling children. She looked down at her little son, so much smaller, it seemed, than nearly all the others, and saw that he was frowning.

'It's sure to be strange at first, George,' she said. 'But I'll be here to fetch you after school. Don't worry.'

'I am not worried, Mother,' said George. 'Merely appalled at the noise and general confusion. How childishly everyone is behaving.'

In Class 5, the reception class, the teacher, who was also new at the school and had never before set eyes on George or any of the other children, was filling in her register. Everyone had been shown a peg to hang their coats on, and a locker to keep their things in, and given a place to sit, and some crayons and paper to draw on. As each new child in turn was called to the teacher's desk, she wrote down their names in the register and, if they knew them, their dates of birth.

'Now then, who are you?' she asked when it was George's turn.

'My name,' said George, 'is George.'

'And do you know when your birthday is, George?'

"It is April the first," said George.

"April Fool's Day," said the teacher smiling.

George did not smile.

"You will find," he said severely, "that I am nobody's fool."

Later, the teacher went round looking at the pictures the children had drawn. Some were of their animals, some of their houses, some of their parents, and one little girl had actually written MUM under her picture.

'That's very good!' said the teacher.

Then she came to George.

If people's eyes could really pop out of their heads, George's new teacher would have gone blind at that instant, for George's picture,

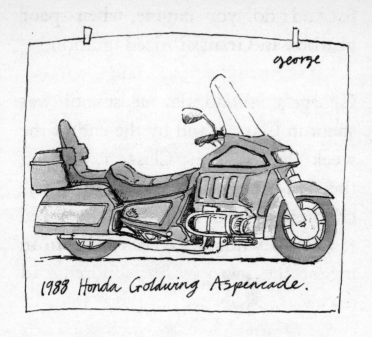

george

1988 Honda Goldwing Aspencade.

minute in detail, was of a motorcycle. Under it was written in joined-up writing,

1988 Honda Goldwing Aspencade.

'George!' gasped the teacher. 'What in the world . . .?'

'I am interested in motorcycles,' said George, 'amongst other things. This is a Japanese tourer. It has a flat

27

four 1182 c.c. engine, a 5-speed gearbox and transistorized ignition.'

George's second day at school was spent in Class 4, and by the end of the week he was in Class 1, among the ten- and eleven-year-olds. The children treated him with the awed respect they might have accorded to an

alien from outer space, and the teachers were, quite simply, flabbergasted.

The headmaster had at first paid little heed to rumours of George's abilities, but that Friday was one that he never forgot.

In the morning, he taught Class 1.

At lunch time, he summoned George to his study.

'Sit down, George,' he said in a kindly voice.

'I can't,' said George.

'Why not?'

'I fear the chair is too high for me,' said George, so the headmaster lifted him on to it.

'Now, George,' he said. 'I just want to ask you some questions. How old are you?'

'Four years and eleven months,' said George.

'They tell me you can do joined-up writing.'

'Up to a point,' said George. 'My physical skills are inferior to my mental abilities.'

'Ah,' said the headmaster in a shaky voice. 'What about numbers?'

'Mathematics, d'you mean?' said George. 'My knowledge is purely in the realm of arithmetic so far. Algebra and geometry are treats in store for me.'

'And reading?' croaked the headmaster.

'Reading,' said George, 'is something I find most enjoyable. There are a great many excellent children's authors published these days, but I must confess to a weakness for the older classics. Take for example *Alice in Wonderland*. What a work of fantasy!'

'Fantastic!' whispered the head-master.

After lunch Class 1 was working on a project about South America, drawing maps and putting in the capital cities and principal rivers and mountain ranges. To be fair to the headmaster, he knew the names of the capitals of most of the countries of South America, but on one he momentarily stumbled.

'The capital of Guyana is . . .' he said. 'Silly of me, it's slipped my mind. Look it up, someone.'

'No need,' said a very young but already familiar voice. 'It's Georgetown.'

That evening George went to bed early.

'I'm quite tired,' he said to his parents

and Laura. 'It's been a busy week.'

'It's amazing,' said his father later. 'To be in the top class, his first week of school!'

'He's top of the top class!' said his mother.

'He's miles cleverer than me!' said Laura proudly. 'He won't need me for help with homework, I'll need him.' George's mother sighed. This time it was a deep sigh of pure regret.

'I just wish he needed me still,' she said. 'He never seems to, now.'

Just then there was an awful wailing from upstairs.

It was a terrified wailing, the cry of a very young child that desperately wants its mother.

'Mummy! Mummy! Mummy!' cried George from the darkness of his bedroom.

'I'm coming, my baby!' called George's mother. 'Mummy's coming!' and she rushed upstairs to find George sitting up in bed, sobbing his heart out. This was not the confident self-assured know-it-all cleverest child in the school. This was just a frightened baby, and she cuddled him as fiercely as she had when he was only tiny and had never spoken a word.

33

'What is it, George darling?' she said as she mopped away his tears. 'Did you have a bad dream?'

'I did, I did, Mummy!' sobbed George.

'What was it? Tell Mummy.'

Gradually George's sobs turned to sniffles, and then he blew his nose and said, 'I dreamt we were doing a science test at school.'

'A science test?'

'Yes, we do science in the new curriculum, you know. And there was a simple question in it that I couldn't answer, and I cried like a baby. I cried in the dream, and I was crying when I woke up. I really must apologize for behaving so childishly.'

'Poor lamb!' said his mother. 'What was the question?'

'It was the order of events in the cycle of the internal combustion engine,' said George.

'Forget about it, George,' said his mother sadly. 'I expect there'll be lots of questions you won't know the answers to.'

'Not if I can help it,' said George.

'Anyway, don't worry. Just go back to sleep. Mummy's here.'

'Oh, I shan't worry any more, Mother,' said George in his usual confident tones. 'I've remembered it now. It's Induction – Compression – Ignition – Exhaust,' and exhausted, he lay back and went happily to sleep.

Carol Singing

Christmas was coming, and one of the teachers was banging away on the piano, as the school practised for the end-of-term service.

'O come, let us adore Him!' sang all one hundred and twenty children.

At any rate one hundred and nineteen of them sang, while the one hundred and twentieth opened her mouth and made a dreadful noise.

'Oh, that voice!' said the head-mistress afterwards, as she drank her coffee in the staffroom. 'You can hear it above all the rest.'

'It's like a cow mooing,' said someone.

'No, more like a pig squealing.'

'Or a dog howling.'

'And to think,' said the headmistress, 'that when that child was born, her parents chose to call her Carol!'

'It's pathetic really,' said Carol's class teacher. 'She loves singing.'

'Singing, you call it?'

'I mean, she loves music. She knows all the words, of all the carols, Carol does.'

'But not the tunes.'

'No, I'm afraid she has absolutely no ear for music.'

'Unfortunately,' said the headmistress, 'we each have two ears and Carol's frightful voice is all I can hear. No matter how nicely the other children sing "I saw three ships come sailing by", all I can hear is that foghorn bellowing its warning of rocks ahead. For goodness' sake, when it comes to the church service, try to get her to keep her voice down.'

'Why don't you keep your voice down?' a catty girl called Catherine was saying to Carol out in the playground.

'I didn't speak,' said Carol.

'I don't mean now. I mean when we're singing. You're awful, you are. You're tone-deaf.'

'What's that mean?' asked Carol.

'It means,' said a know-all girl called Noelle, 'that you can't tell differences in musical pitch. I've got perfect pitch, I have.'

'It sounds all right inside my head,' Carol said.

'Well, keep it in there,' they said. 'Don't let it out to give everyone else a headache.'

It had always been the same. It wasn't too bad when Carol first went to school, because quite a few of the infants weren't all that good at singing in tune. But as time passed and they all grew older, everyone else seemed to get the hang of it. Of course not all of the children had good voices, but they all seemed to rub along all right and those that weren't brilliant at least had the sense to sing softly.

But not Carol. She liked to keep going full blast, and if she ever hit a right note, it was a complete fluke.

The day of the carol service dawned, and Carol's teacher watched anxiously as the children came in through the classroom door. It's not nice of me, she thought, but if only Carol could have a cold today, the kind that makes you lose your voice. But there was no such luck.

'Sing a bit quietly today, Carol, won't you?' the teacher said before they set out.

'Why?'

'Well, you do . . . shout a bit.'

But even though the church was full of mums and dads and grandparents and many others as well as all the children, and even though her teacher had put Carol at the very far end of a pew and behind a large pillar, still she could clearly be heard through all the singing.

Some people were amused and smiled, some frowned angrily, several babies burst out crying, and one of the grandfathers switched off his hearing aid, as, through carol after carol, there sounded the drones and groans and moans of that awful voice.

'It isn't as if she was just a bit sharp or flat,' said know-all Noelle afterwards. 'She's just absolutely tuneless.'

'Oh, I don't know,' said catty Catherine. 'She wasn't too bad on the Amens,' and they went off together, giggling.

Carol walked home alone, wondering for the thousandth time why it was that, though she could hear the tunes clearly in her mind, they came out all wrong.

'I *wish* I could sing properly,' she said, and then she had an idea.

'Why shouldn't I be taught?' she said. 'After all, you can be taught anything – how to read, how to write, how to do sums, and later on things like how to drive a car. Why can't you be taught to sing?'

So as soon as she got home, she opened the Yellow Pages.

SINGING TUITION (she found) see MUSIC TEACHERS

There were several names under this heading, and one was in the very next street to hers. She went to find her mother.

'Mum,' she said. 'Can I have singing lessons?'

'Why?' said Carol's mother. What's the use, she thought.

'I just want to learn to sing in tune, that's all. I can hear the music in my head, but when I open my mouth, it comes out all funny.'

'I know, dear.'

'And look, there's a music teacher in the next street, Mum,' said Carol, and she pointed to the place in the Yellow Pages.

'Who's going to pay for these lessons?' asked her mother.

'Me. I'll save up. Honest. Can I have them? Please?'

'We'd better go and see,' said Carol's mother.

So next morning, a Saturday, they went together to a little house in the next street and knocked on the door. On it was a notice

MISS N. CHANTER
MUSIC TEACHER

It was opened by a little old lady with grey hair done in a bun and the nicest, smiliest sort of face.

'Hullo,' she said. 'What can I do for you?'

'My daughter wants singing lessons,' said Carol's mother. 'How much do you charge?'

'That depends,' said Miss N. Chanter. 'Come in, and we'll see.'

She led them into a small room mostly filled by a large piano, on top of which a black cat lay sleeping.

Miss N. Chanter sat down at the piano.

'Now then,' she said, 'what's your name?'

'Carol.'

'Hm. Do you like music?'

'Oh yes! I like all sorts of music and I know loads of different tunes. I can hear them all in my head perfectly, but when I open my mouth they don't come out quite right. I just want to be able to sing properly, like everyone else at school.'

'Well, let's try,' said Miss N. Chanter, and she played the first few bars of 'God save the Queen'.

'Know the words?' she said.

'Oh yes!'

'OK. Let's go. One . . . two . . .'

'Well, well,' said Miss N. Chanter after the last quavering 'Queen' had died away and the black cat had dashed from the room with all his fur standing on end, 'I see what you mean, Carol. Or rather I hear what you mean. We have problems.'

'You mean you can't teach me?' said Carol.

'I didn't say that.'

'You mean it's going to cost a lot of money?' said Carol's mother.

'I didn't say that either. In fact, if I can't teach Carol to sing, I won't charge you a penny.'

That's all right then, thought Carol's mother, she hasn't got a hope.

So they fixed that Carol should come by herself for her first lesson in a week's time.

'I've had an idea!' was the first thing Miss N. Chanter said when she opened the door to Carol on the next Saturday morning. 'I believe you when you say you can hear tunes in your head but it's what comes out of your mouth that's the trouble. Now, if we could catch the tunes on their way out . . .'

'I don't understand,' said Carol.

Miss N. Chanter put her hand in

the pocket of her woolly cardigan and took out a small mouth-organ. She held it out to Carol.

'Try this,' she said.

'But I can't play any instrument,' said Carol.

'This isn't just any instrument. Try playing a tune on it. Low notes on the left, high notes on the right. All you've got to do is blow and suck. Go on.'

Carol hesitated. This is silly, she

50

thought, I've never played a mouth-organ before. It will just be a horrid noise, and, as though she had spoken out loud, Miss N. Chanter said, 'No, it won't. Choose something simple, a nursery rhyme, say. How about "Pop Goes the Weasel", know the tune of that? Right then, just sing it in your head and suck and blow.'

Just what it was that made her move the mouth-organ to left or to right or told her when to suck and when to blow Carol never could afterwards understand. But she never forgot the playing of that first simple little tune. Every note was right. No one could have played "Pop Goes the Weasel" better. Even the black cat purred loudly.

'I thought as much,' said Miss N. Chanter. 'It's just a question of catching the melody that's in your head before it gets out into the open air. Now choose another tune.'

So Carol chose 'Widecombe Fair' and the tune came out perfectly, every bit of it, old Uncle Tom Cobley and all!

Carol took the mouth-organ out of her mouth and stared at it in wonder.

'It's magic!' she said.

'You could say that,' said Miss N. Chanter.

'It's wonderful,' said Carol, 'but . . .'

'But what?'

'. . . but how will it teach me to sing?'

Miss N. Chanter sat down at the piano and played the scale of C Major.

Then with one finger she struck middle C.

'Play that,' she said.

Carol played it.

'Now this time,' said Miss N. Chanter, 'I'll hit the note again, you play it, and then quickly take the thing out of your mouth and sing it – "Lah".'

And it worked! Carol sang the perfect middle C!

After that it was plain sailing.

At the second lesson Carol could

play a scale on the mouth-organ and then she was managing without the mouth-organ, singing to Miss N. Chanter's accompaniment on the piano, and by the end of the tenth lesson she could sing any tune unaccompanied.

'That's it, then, Carol,' said Miss N. Chanter. 'You can sing. And what's more, you've a very good voice.'

'It's all thanks to you and your mouth-organ,' said Carol. 'Please, how much do I owe you?'

'Oh, we'll see about that,' said Miss N. Chanter. 'Now let's have one last song. How about "Over the Rainbow"? D'you know that?'

'Oh yes!' cried Carol. 'How funny you should choose that! We're going to do *The Wizard of Oz* for the school concert this term.'

'Fancy!' said Miss N. Chanter. 'Tell you what, Carol. If you get the part of Dorothy, I won't charge you a penny.'

'Who's going to play Dorothy?' said the headmistress to the teacher who was organizing the concert.

'Oh, Noelle, I should think,' said the teacher. 'She's got perfect pitch and not a bad voice. There are a number of girls who might be good enough. I'll have an audition.'

'Don't bother with Carol,' the headmistress said, and everybody laughed.

You can guess the rest, can't you?

Half a dozen girls tried for the part of Dorothy, and know-all Noelle was maybe the best. But before she could be told so, one more girl had come into the room.

'What are you doing here, Carol?' the teacher said. 'We're auditioning for *The Wizard of Oz*, you know.'

'She could make the noises for the Cowardly Lion,' said catty Catherine, and the others sniggered.

'Please,' said Carol. 'I want to be Dorothy.'

'Carol must have the part beyond the shadow of a doubt,' said the teacher to the headmistress afterwards. 'She put me in mind of the young Judy Garland. She sang "Over the Rainbow" quite beautifully. She'll bring the house down!'

'I cannot understand it,' said the headmistress. 'It smacks of witchcraft.'

And you won't be surprised to hear that, at the end of the school concert, among the clapping, cheering audience that stood to applaud the wonderful singing of Carol as Dorothy in *The Wizard of Oz* was a little old lady with grey hair done in a bun and the nicest, smiliest sort of face.

Maisie Grazer

You don't expect a name to *mean* anything, do you?

Someone called Baker doesn't necessarily grow up to make bread, nor does a Barber have to cut hair, and if your name is Smellie, it doesn't mean you are.

So no one thought there was anything odd when a Mr Grazer married a Miss Meadows.

After a while Mrs Grazer had a baby, a little girl, and they called her Maisie.

A very normal baby was Maisie Grazer, or so it seemed at first. It was not till Maisie's mother started her on solid foods that the Grazers noticed anything strange.

'It's funny,' said Mrs Grazer to her husband. 'Maisie doesn't seem to like the usual baby foods — liver-and-bacon, minced beef, lamb casserole, that sort of thing. She won't eat any of them.'

'Maybe she doesn't like the meat in them,' said Mr Grazer. 'Perhaps she's going to be a vegetarian.'

'You're joking,' said Mrs Grazer, but all the same she bought some Purée of Spinach, and Maisie gollopped it down. In fact she seemed to like it so much that she spoke her first word.

'Moo,' she said.

'Did you hear that?' cried Mrs Grazer. 'She said "More"!'

'It sounded like "Moo" to me,' said Mr Grazer.

'Don't be silly,' said Mrs Grazer. 'Only cows say "Moo".'

After the Purée of Spinach, Mrs Grazer bought some Mixed Young

Vegetables and tried them on Maisie the following day. Maisie gollopped them down.

'Maa,' she said.

'Did you hear that?' cried Mrs Grazer. 'She said "More"!'

'It sounded like "Maa" to me,' said Mr Grazer.

'Don't be silly,' said Mrs Grazer. 'Only sheep say "Maa".'

Time passed, and though Maisie Grazer still turned her little nose up at anything to do with meat in it, she seemed to be thriving. Soon, though she still said nothing but 'Moo' or 'Maa', she began to crawl.

The weather was beautiful, and one sunny day Mrs Grazer spread a rug on the little lawn outside and laid

Maisie on it. No sooner had she done so than the front door bell rang.

By the time Mrs Grazer returned from collecting the post, Maisie had crawled to the edge of the rug. But it was not this that nearly made Mrs Grazer's eyes pop out of her head. It was what the baby was doing!

Hastily she snatched her up and hurried indoors.

'What's the matter?' said Mr Grazer when he came back from work that evening. 'You look worried stiff. What's up?'

'It's Maisie,' said Mrs Grazer.

'What about her? She's not ill?'

'No. It's what she was doing, this morning, on the lawn.'

'What was she doing?'

'She was eating grass.'

Mr Grazer laughed.

'Is that all?' he said. 'You had me worried for a moment. Babies are always picking things up and stuffing them in their mouths, you know that. What's a blade or two of grass?'

'It wasn't like that,' said Mrs Grazer in a low voice.

Fuss about nothing, thought Mr Grazer, and he picked up his daughter and carried her out on to the lawn and put her down.

He stood watching, smiling at his wife's groundless fears, but after some moments the smile was replaced by a look of horror, and the colour drained from his cheeks.

'Phone the doctor!' he cried to his wife, scooping Maisie up again. 'Quickly!'

'Now then,' said the doctor when

he arrived, 'who is it that's ill in the Grazer family? The baby looks a picture. Her vegetarian diet seems to be suiting her. You can't have called me out to see her. But you look a bit under the weather, Mr Grazer. And so indeed do you, Mrs Grazer. Which of you is poorly?'

'Neither,' said Mr Grazer.

'It's Maisie,' said Mrs Grazer.

'It's what she's been doing,' they said.

'What's she been doing?' said the doctor.

'Eating grass.'

The doctor laughed.

'That's nothing to worry about,' he said. 'Babies are always picking things up and stuffing them in their mouths. A blade or two of grass won't hurt her.'

64

'It wasn't a blade or two,' they said.

Fuss about nothing, thought the doctor, and he picked up Maisie and carried her out on to the lawn and put her down.

Without hesitation she dropped her head, opened her mouth, and began to graze. Jaws moving rhythmically, Maisie Grazer crawled slowly along, tearing off the juicy green grass with occasional cries of 'Moo!' or 'Maa!'

until she reached the far edge of the lawn. Behind her stretched a narrow swath of mown ground.

Mrs Grazer ran to pick the baby up and wipe the green stains from her mouth.

'You see, Doctor?' she said.

The doctor nodded.

'Ever known such a thing before, Doctor?' asked Mr Grazer.

The doctor shook his head.

'What d'you think, Doctor?' they said.

'Mr and Mrs Grazer,' said the doctor solemnly, 'I think that your daughter is living up to her name. Such a condition is unknown in medical history. It would appear to me that you are the parents of, and I the doctor attendant on, the world's first grazing baby.'

66

'But what will it do to her?' they cried.

'That,' said the doctor, 'remains to be seen. Ring me if you need me, otherwise I will call back tomorrow, and in the meantime, wherever you put her, keep off the grass!'

On the following morning the doctor arrived at the Grazers' house very early indeed, so excited was he at this unique case. Would the baby have sicked up its unnatural meal? Would it have a badly upset stomach? Why had the parents not phoned him?

'Why haven't you phoned me?' he said as soon as they opened the door.

'No need,' said Mr Grazer.

'You mean the baby slept the night through?'

'Like a lamb,' said Mrs Grazer.

'Never had a bleat out of her,' said Mr Grazer.

'Amazing!' said the doctor. 'Has she had her breakfast yet?'

'No.'

'Well, I wonder ... do you think ... in the interests of medical science ... that is, seeing that it seems to have done her no harm ... look here, would you consider, while I'm here, putting her out on the lawn again?'

So they did, and once again Maisie Grazer lowered her little head and opened her little mouth and with her sharp little teeth grazed another swath across the lawn.

'Remarkable!' said the doctor. 'As a matter of interest, just for the record, how many teeth has she?'

'Six,' said Mrs Grazer proudly.

'Imagine!' said the doctor. They

walked back to the house, passing the garden shed in which Mr Grazer kept his lawn-mower.

'Tell you what,' said the doctor, pointing at it. 'Once she's got all thirty-two, you won't need that again.'

And how right he was.

Once Maisie Grazer was old enough, there was never any further need for her father to mow the lawn on a Saturday morning. He could sit in his deckchair with his paper and a cup of coffee, while his daughter did the work. Like all babies she progressed from crawling to toddling to walking to running, but to graze of course she must needs revert to crawling, and by the time she was ten or eleven she could cut the whole lawn in one go. Working methodically from

side to side, she left it as neatly pat-
terned with parallel stripes as the most
expensive machine.

Meat, you will not be surprised to
hear, Maisie Grazer never touched,
but though grass remained her
favourite food, her remarkable powers
of digestion allowed her to eat any
greenstuff raw.

At mealtimes in the Grazer household the father and mother would sit down at table in the normal manner, while out in the garden Maisie would chew on a cabbage or two or munch on a lettuce for lunch.

Sometimes the family doctor, passing on his rounds, would stop his car to look through the fence and smile in smug self-satisfaction at the sight of Maisie among the greenstuff.

'May I live long enough,' he would say to himself, 'to see how her children turn out.'

And he did, for when she was twenty-one, Maisie Grazer married and changed her name, though not her habits. Indeed the honeymoon (in the spring, when the young grass is at its tenderest) was spent in the rich grazing lands of the West Country, where the indulgent young husband could lie at ease and watch his bride, as on hands and knees she munched her way across a field of clover, uttering muffled 'Moos' or 'Maas'.

And a year or so later, Maisie herself became a mother.

How anxiously and with what interest did Mr and Mrs Grazer watch the progress of their grandson, especially when he was first offered solid foods.

As indeed did the old family doctor.

But greatly to the relief of the grandparents and much to the disappointment of the medical man, the baby gollopped down liver-and-bacon or minced beef or lamb casserole, but would not look at Purée of Spinach or Mixed Young Vegetables, and never – throughout his life indeed

– could be persuaded to eat cabbage or lettuce. He just loved meat, all sorts of meat and lots of it.

As for grass, that was for him something to be crawled on, toddled on, walked on, run on, but not – ever – eaten.

But then of course he wasn't a Grazer.

Oh sorry – I forgot to tell you that the man Maisie married was called Butcher. Not that he was one of course, but then you don't expect a name to *mean* anything, do you?

Banger

Steven did love sausages!

To say that they were his favourite food was not enough. Steven had sausages all the time. He had them for breakfast, lunch, tea and supper. He had big sausages, short fat ones and long thin ones, pork sausages, beef sausages, Cumberland sausages, chipolatas, saveloys, salami and frankfurters. He ate them fried, boiled, baked, grilled or smoked, hot or cold. And it wasn't simply that Steven had sausages for every meal, every day of every week of every year – oh no, it was more than that. He had sausages with everything he ate.

At breakfast time he would put cornflakes and sugar and milk on a sausage, then eat a sausage with bacon and eggs, and then slice a sausage down the middle and spread each half with butter and jam. You can guess what Steven always began with at lunch and at supper, but for afters he might have rice pudding and sausage, sausage and custard, sausage dumplings with treacle, or perhaps best of all, a vanilla ice-cream cornet with a sausage stuck in the top of it. As for

75

tea, well there were always sausages on hot buttered toast, and perhaps chocolate éclairs with a sausage on each, or just simply sausage-meat sandwiches. And of course Steven never stirred his tea with a spoon if there was a sausage handy.

'Don't you think,' said Steven's father one day (it was funny, he hated sausages), 'that you ought to put Steven on a diet? Or at least make him give up those . . . things?' (He could not bring himself to say the word.)

'Oh I couldn't,' said Steven's mother from the cooker. 'He does love sausages.'

She turned a row of chipolatas on to their other sides.

Steven's father frowned.

'Have you noticed,' he said, 'what the boy's beginning to look like?' and he went out of the room.

Now most babies do look a bit like sausages when they're very small, but, as they grow bigger, arms and legs and necks begin to stick out of them more, and their bodies are not so plump. This had never happened with Steven. Rather than growing less like a sausage, he had grown more like one.

Steven's mother looked carefully at her son as he rolled into the kitchen. I see what his father means, she thought. Steven's arms and legs weren't really noticeable compared with the size of his body. And he had no neck to speak of, but his head sat on the end of it just like that bit that sometimes comes out of the end of a sausage, she realized. But it was the look of his skin that suddenly worried her. How stretched it was, how brown, how shiny, how greasy! She watched him chopping chipolatas over his porridge.

'Steven,' she said. 'Don't you think three's enough to start with?'

'No,' he said, chopping up a fourth.

'One of these days you'll burst,' she said nervously.

'Like a sausage does,' asked Steven, 'if you forget to stick a fork in it?'

'Yes,' said his mother. 'It gives a little squeak, and a little gurgle, and a little bang.'

'Got my eggs ready?' said Steven with his mouth full. 'I'm hungry.'

Wearily, his mother turned back to the frying-pan.

Two eggs on fried bread and three rashers of bacon (and of course more of Steven's favourite food) followed the chipolatas-and-porridge, and he was just dipping a big pork sausage into the honey-pot when the phone rang in the hall.

While his mother was talking, she

thought that there was a kind of groaning noise coming from the kitchen. She put the phone down and listened.

'Mum!' cried Steven. 'Stick a fork in me! Quick!'

And then she heard a big squeak, and a big gurgle, and a big BANG!

Steven did *love* sausages.

Poor Edgar

'Poor Edgar,' said Victoria.

'He was very old,' said Alice.

'What did he die of?' said Helena.

'Just being old, I should think,' said Louise.

'How old was he?' said Beatrice.

The five sisters stood staring at the dead guinea-pig, lying on the floor of his hutch. He looked flat.

'Let me think,' said Victoria, the eldest. 'We got him when I was five and now I'm eleven – that makes him six. That's a long life. No wonder he's died.'

The eyes of Beatrice, the youngest, filled with tears and she gave a loud snorting sob.

'Don't cry, Bee,' said Alice. 'He's all right, he's gone to Heaven.'

'It's not that,' gulped Beatrice. 'It's just . . . I don't want to die.'

'Well, why should you?' said Helena.

'Because I'm six. Vicky said that's a long life.'

'For a guinea-pig, she meant,' said Louise.

Beatrice sniffed and Victoria mopped at her.

'Cheer up,' she said. 'We'll give him a lovely funeral, shall we? I'll dig the hole, and Alice, you and Helena make a cross to go on his grave, and Louise, you take Bee and pick some flowers.'

Digging the hole, under the weeping willow tree at the bottom of the garden, took quite a long time. The spade was a bit big for Victoria and

the job was harder than she'd thought it would be. The earth kept falling back in again, and the others were ready long before she was.

Louise had a posy of forget-me-nots ('because we won't,' she said) and Beatrice had picked a lot of dandelion flowers ('because he liked them') and Alice and Helena had made a cross out of two bits of board. On it Alice had written with a felt marker

EDGAR
AGED 6
R.I.P.

'What does R.I.P. mean?' said Beatrice.

'It's what you put on graves,' they said.

'It means "Rest in Peace",' said Victoria, leaning on her spade.

'We ought to have put "Rest in Peace Edgar",' said Alice, and she changed it to R.I.P.E.

Victoria dug out a last spadeful.

'Come on,' she said. 'We'll go and fetch him now.'

'I want to carry him,' said Alice.

'No, me,' said Helena.

'Why can't I?' said Louise.

Beatrice's eyes filled with tears.

'What's the matter now?' they said.

'I don't want to.'

'Don't want to what?'

'Carry him.'

'Well, you needn't,' said Victoria, getting out of the hole. 'The rest of us will be the pall-bearers.'

'What's a pall-bearer?' said Alice and Helena and Louise.

'Someone who carries the coffin.'

'But we haven't got a coffin.'

'Nor we have. That's the next thing to do. We'll find a box and put Edgar in it, and then the four of us can hold a corner each.'

'What about me?' said Beatrice.

'You can be the undertaker and walk behind the coffin.'

Beatrice sniffed.

'I don't want to be the undertaker,' she said.

'Well, what do you want then?'

'I want to be the overtaker.'

'Oh, all right,' said Victoria. 'Call it what you want.'

'But don't start crying again,' said Alice.

'And dry your eyes,' said Helena.

'And blow your nose,' said Louise.

'Come on,' said Victoria. 'Let's go and see what we can find.'

In the garden shed they found an

apple-box. It had a label on it with pictures of lovely juicy red apples.

'Edgar liked them,' said Beatrice in a voice of deepest gloom.

'Well then, it'll be just right for his coffin,' said Victoria.

'Wonder why it's called a coffin?' said Alice.

'Perhaps,' said Helena, 'because people used to die of having a bad cough.'

'Edgar didn't,' said Louise.

Beatrice's eyes filled with tears again.

At last the funeral procession was ready to start.

They had strewn fresh grass on the bed of the apple-box and laid the body

of Edgar reverently upon it, and nailed on the lid.

Alice closed the door of the empty hutch.

'Shall we be able to have another guinea-pig?' she said.

'Or two perhaps?' said Helena.

'They'd be company for each other,' said Louise.

'They cost an awful lot,' said Victoria.

'I've got 10p,' said Beatrice.

'10p!' said Victoria. 'We'd need more like £10 to get two guinea-pigs. We'll just have to save up, that's all. Now then, are you all ready?'

Solemnly the funeral procession made its way down to the weeping willow tree. The four elder girls each held a corner of the apple-box and the overtaker marched behind them, wearing a kind of black bonnet made from a bin liner. All wore black arm-bands of the same material.

They halted at the graveside and carefully lowered the apple-box. It just fitted into the grave but it was obvious that the hole was much too shallow.

'I'll have to make it deeper,' said Victoria.

They took the coffin out again and she set to work.

Another six inches down the spade clinked upon something. Victoria bent and picked up a small round object.

'What is it?' asked the pall-bearers.

'A coin, I think. It's all covered in muck and stuff.'

'See if there are any more.'

Victoria dug around, but there weren't.

Beatrice gave a sob.

'What's the matter, Bee?' they said.

'Can't we put Edgar in the hole now?' she said. 'I don't like frunerals. They make me very very sad.'

'Oh, all right,' said Victoria. 'It's probably only a 2p piece by the size of it anyway,' and she put the thing in the pocket of her jeans.

Then they lowered the coffin once more into the grave.

'We ought to say something,' said Helena.

'Like "Dust to dust and ashes to ashes",' said Alice.

'Can't we just say "Goodbye, Edgar"?' said Louise.

So they all said it, except Beatrice, whose heart was too full for speech, and then they piled the earth on top of the apple-box, and set on the mound the cross with its inscription

EDGAR
AGED 6
R.I.P.E.

and arranged the forget-me-nots and the dandelion flowers around it.

'Edgar has died,' said the girls' mother to her husband when he arrived home from work. 'They gave him a splendid funeral.'

They all went down to the grave, and their father read the inscription on the cross.

'Well, he did live to a ripe old age,' he said.

Beatrice snorted, and Victoria, reaching into her pocket for a handkerchief, suddenly remembered the coin she had found.

She brought it out.

'Look, Dad,' she said. 'I found this when I was digging. What d'you think it is?'

'Let's take it indoors and clean it up a bit,' her father said.

As he was doing so, he suddenly let out a whistle of amazement.

'This is a gold coin!' he said, and when he had scraped at it a bit more,

'It's a guinea!'

'Is that what you use for buying guinea-pigs?' asked Beatrice.

'You could buy an awful lot of them with this, I should think. Guineas must be quite valuable because they stopped making them ages ago, nearly two hundred years, I should think. Let's see if we can make out the date on it. Yes, here it is. 1815. The year of the battle of Waterloo! I'll take it in to that coin-dealer in town tomorrow and get it valued.'

The five girls were all waiting at the gate when their father arrived home the following evening.

'Did you get it valued?' they said.

'Yes.'

'Is it enough to buy two guinea-pigs?' said Victoria.

'What would they cost?'

'About ten pounds.'

'It's worth much more than that.'

'Twenty pounds?' said Alice.

'No, more.'

'Fifty?' said Helena.

'More than that.'

'A hundred pounds,' said Louise. 'It couldn't be worth more than a hundred pounds.'

'The coin dealer,' said her father slowly, 'has offered to buy your

Waterloo guinea for . . . five hundred pounds!'

'Wow!' shouted all the girls. Even Beatrice was beaming broadly.

'And just think,' their father said. 'None of this would have happened if Edgar hadn't died.'

Beatrice's face began to crumple.

'Oh, Dad,' murmured Victoria. 'You shouldn't have said that.'

'Poor Edgar!' howled Beatrice. 'Poor poor Edgar!'